Deep in the Underworld

PRAISE FOR *STORYSHARES*

"One of the brightest innovators and game-changers in the education industry."
– Forbes

"Your success in applying research-validated practices to promote literacy serves as a valuable model for other organizations seeking to create evidence-based literacy programs."

- Library of Congress

"We need powerful social and educational innovation, and Storyshares is breaking new ground. The organization addresses critical problems facing our students and teachers. I am excited about the strategies it brings to the collective work of making sure every student has an equal chance in life."
– Teach For America

"Around the world, this is one of the up-and-coming trailblazers changing the landscape of literacy and education."
- International Literacy Association

"It's the perfect idea. There's really nothing like this. I mean wow, this will be a wonderful experience for young people."   - Andrea Davis Pinkney, Executive Director, Scholastic

"Reading for meaning opens opportunities for a lifetime of learning. Providing emerging readers with engaging texts that are designed to offer both challenges and support for each individual will improve their lives for years to come. Storyshares is a wonderful start."
- David Rose, Co-founder of CAST & UDL

Deep in the Underworld

Caroline Gee

STORYSHARES

Story Share, Inc.
New York. Boston. Philadelphia

Published in the United States by Story Share, Inc.

Storyshares
Story Share, Inc.
24 N. Bryn Mawr Avenue #340
Bryn Mawr, PA 19010-3304
www.storyshares.org

Inspiring reading with a new kind of book.

Interest Level: Middle School
Grade Level Equivalent: 3.1

9781642611472

Book design by Storyshares

Printed in the United States of America

Storyshares Presents

1

Nico was getting tired of the silence. It was all around him in the cold, chilly air, drifting over the flat, bare plains. He had been walking for miles—past the Fields of Asphodel, past his father's palace.

Nico shivered as he walked, and wrapped his old aviator jacket more tightly around his shoulders. People expected him to feel right at home in the Underworld (his father was Hades, after all), but whenever he got this far from his father's palace, he felt anxious and insecure.

Maybe part of the reason was that his father had sent him on an impossible mission: to find the Doors of Death and set them free.

It was all the fault of the evil Earth goddess, Gaea. The Doors of Death were the hidden passageway between the Underworld and the mortal world. Because she had chained down the Doors, Gaea controlled who could and could not pass through them. Thanks to her, filthy monsters that had only just been killed could go straight back to earth.

Just thinking about it made Nico's insides twist. He kept walking, though, determined to fulfill his father's command. I have to do this, he told himself. He would find the Doors of Death, he would break the chains, and he would defeat Gaea, if it was the last thing he did.

He had been so absorbed in his thinking that he didn't notice he had wandered into a small cavern. It wasn't until his shoulder bumped against the stone wall that he realized.

Where am I?

He looked around, trying to remember if he had ever been here before. It looked vaguely familiar. The narrow cavern walls, the sloping floor, the sharp chill.

Suddenly, Nico knew where he was.

He turned and walked back the way he had come, up the slope to where the air wasn't so cold. He could feel his heart pounding, could hear his thoughts buzzing. If he'd kept going along that narrow path, he would have entered a large cavern, with a giant chasm cutting down the middle of it: Tartarus.

Nico got chills just thinking about it. He remembered the last time he had entered that cavern. He had stood at the edge of the chasm for a long time before turning away. He remembered the cold, dark feeling, the horrible power that rose from the hole like a foul breath.

No one had ever entered Tartarus and returned—for obvious reasons. It was the place deep, deep below the earth, "as far beneath Hades as heaven is high above the Earth," as Zeus put it. In that deep pit, thousands of dead monsters re-formed and roamed free. Entering Tartarus would mean signing your own death warrant.

I'm glad to be out of there, Nico thought... but a very different thought made him spin around. The Doors of Death! They could be anywhere in the Underworld—including Tartarus. It made sense. Hiding the Doors in the deepest part of the Underworld seemed exactly like something Gaea would do.

But... Nico's stomach turned at the thought of venturing into that frozen pit. He remembered the monsters, thirsting for demigod blood. Most of all, he worried about getting back out once he entered Tartarus. What if he got stuck there forever?

I'm a son of Hades, Nico reminded himself. He had been developing his powers for years. Surely he was powerful enough to at least sneak into Tartarus and escape again.

And if the Doors of Death really were down there, then all of Nico's hard work and sacrifice would be worth it.

Nico took a deep breath and headed into Tartarus.

2

Now that he knew where he was going, everything seemed magnified. The bitter coldness. The heavy darkness. The eerie sense of menace as he passed through the tunnel. His head felt light, and his limbs were weak.

The path opened wide. Nico entered the cavern.

Gods of Olympus! The giant chasm screamed of blood and death and fear. He could sense the power rising from it.

Nico slowly stepped forward. He could hear himself breathing. He couldn't imagine going down into the pit. But the Doors of Death...

"It's now or never," he told himself. Racing forward, he leaped into the chasm.

Time didn't seem to exist anymore. All there was around him was the black darkness and the wind whistling in his ears.

He had no idea how long he had been falling. It took all of his self-control to keep from screaming.

The darkness seemed to close in on him, as though the chasm walls were narrowing. He was afraid this place would suffocate him.

He took deep breaths, trying to calm his screaming nerves. He had expected cold, but the air here was hot. Was Tartarus a dessert, then? A steaming rock? Whatever it was, it definitely wouldn't be pleasant. Although Tartarus was the birthplace of monsters, it was also their prison.

The chances of his escaping alive were slim, close to impossible. But there was no turning back now.

The air turned hotter and the awful smell of rotten eggs filled Nico's nostrils. He had passed through the narrow chasm, into a vast cavern. Below him were black plains, mountains of rock, and fiery craters. Directly below him, jagged rocks awaited. They looked very sharp.

There was nothing for him to grab onto, no nearby ledge or foothold. His sword was useless to him now. If he hit those rocks, he could die instantly, demigod or not.

But wait. Something big and green was galloping across the plain, coming toward where he would land. It was a monster: a kind of giant lizard on horse's legs. In less than a minute, he'd be speared on a rock and eaten like a shish kebab!

Nico went limp with terror. Before he could hit the sharp blade of rock, though, something long and green slapped him back up into the air.

The world spun wildly around him. He started to fall again—but before he could reach the rocks, he found himself caught in the grip of a long, scaly tail. The monster had plucked him out of the air and wrapped its tail around him.If he could reach his sword, he could defend himself. But the creature had him wrapped in such a tight grip, he couldn't move his arms. He could barely breathe.

3

The monster set him down on the ground, and watched him. It slowly opened and closed its jaws, revealing two rows of sharp teeth. The tail that had caught Nico waved menacingly in the air.

The monster roared, deafeningly, and flared the frills decorating its neck. Nico drew his sword, but knew he couldn't win a fight against this creature.

Nico tried to get to his feet. His head hurt, his chest ached, his throat was dry, and every part in his body felt bruised and sore. He peered back up at the monster.

"Drakon," Nico whispered.

Nico turned, ready to run for his life, but found his path blocked by two hideous cyclops. They were armed and disgusting, with gray rags for clothes and skin sagging with fat. One had a tangle of bright, red hair above his one eye. The other sprouted curly, black hair. Their skin was the color of copper. The two creatures cackled, and showed sharp yellow teeth. They raised their clubs and approached Nico.

"Demigod," they growled. "Yes, we know what you are. We smelled you from afar. Gaea will be pleased. Maybe she'll let us have a bite of your flesh!"

Nico swallowed hard. He raised his sword and pointed it at them. "Don't come any closer!" he shouted.

They laughed at him. "A dainty meal you'll make!"

They began to advance. Nico darted glances this way and that. Behind him, the way was blocked by the huge green dragon. In front, two cyclops were waving their weapons.

There was no way Nico could fight all three monsters and defeat them. There only one way to survive this. He would have to talk his way out.

Everyone knew cyclops were as dumb as doorknobs. He'd heard of other demigods who had ticked them and lived to tell the tale. Maybe he could do the same.

He stood tall, and tried to look confident, unafraid. "So, who's this Gaea?" he asked in a slow drawl, even though he knew plenty well who she was.

"She is our master!" the cyclops roared. "She is the mother of all cyclops! Our savior, our hero! She will destroy all demigods in the universe!"

"That's... nice," Nico said, smiling weakly. "So, uh, what are you guys doing here?"

The two cyclops paused, confused.

"We must bring you to Gaea," they said. "She requires two demigods. Then we can eat you."

Nico racked his brain for a way to trick them.

"But I'm one demigod, not two," Nico said. "Won't she be mad if you show up with only half of what she wants?"

The cyclops both raged. "She will rip our flesh and snap our bones," the red-haired one screamed. "Then we will die again and I will have to re- form again and I will have to find another T-shirt again!" He gestured at the smelly rag hanging from his shoulders.

"Shut up, fool!" the other cyclops snarled. "I will have to repair my skin for the eighth time!"

"We should just eat him now and never tell Gaea about him," the first one grunted. "I'll take the legs!"

"Woah, woah, woah!" Nico backed away from the cyclops. "Boys, boys. I see my disguise fooled you. I'm not really a demigod. I'm a monster, like you!"

"No way," the red head said. "You smell like a demigod. Like buttery bread!"

"That's part of the disguise!" Nico protested. The idea had suddenly popped in his head, and now that he had said it, there was no way he could take it back. "I trick demigods into thinking I'm one of them. And I suck their souls into my sword!"

He raised his dark, Stygian weapon and let them examine it from a safe distance.

"I don't believe you!" the black-haired cyclops roared. He turned to his friend and said, "He smells exactly like a demigod!"

"Uh, well actually," Nico searched his brain for something to say. "It's my cologne. See, I have this hot girlfriend. She's an awesome monster, but she has a thing for demigods. So I wear this cologne. She can't resist."

The two cyclops thought about this, with matching moronic expressions on their faces. Finally, they both said, "Ohhhh."

All of a sudden, Nico found himself hanging out with a pair of one-eyed friends.

4

They introduced themselves as Willy and Philly.

"Can I see the demigod souls?" Willy asked. He was the black-haired one. "In your sword? Please?"

Nico laughed. A minute ago, these cyclops had threatened to eat him. Now, they were saying, "Please."

Nico raised his sword and took a deep breath. He closed his eyes. He had realized recently that his sword absorbed energy from the souls in the Fields of Asphodel. If he concentrated hard enough, he could pull some of that energy out of the sword.

After a moment, Nico heard gasps of admiration from the two cyclops. When he opened his eyes, he saw a whirlpool of dark tendrils rippling outwards from his sword. Every now and then, the outline of a face would form in the dark swirls before fading away. "It's pretty!" Philly exclaimed. "Can we eat it?"

Nico laughed again. "No, but maybe you could answer some questions for me."

In chorus, the cyclops said, "Sure!"

Nico jerked his head toward the drakon behind him. "Is that monster yours?"

The cyclops nodded. "Yes, that's Bloodsucker, our most faithful pet."

Nico felt a bit lightheaded, imagining all the blood the drakon must have sucked. "Hey, here's another question. What do you guys know about the Doors of Death?"

Both cyclops perked up.

Red-haired Philly said, "plenty," before Willy interrupted him.

"Sorry, we can't tell you," Willy said. "Gaea warned us about telling her secrets to strangers."

"I'm not a stranger!" Nico protested. "I'm your friend! Your new best bud! You can tell your BFF anything!"

Willy frowned. "BFF?" he stammered. "What's a BFF?"

"Never mind, it doesn't matter," Nico said. "The point is, you guys can trust me. I was just curious about where the Doors are. I've heard a lot about them."

The cyclops shared an uncomfortable glance. Hesitantly, Willy said, "I guess I could tell you a little."

"The Doors of Death are chained down in the Dark Lands," Philly blurted out.

"The Dark Lands?" The words made Nico queasy. "What's that?"

"It's where all the most powerful monsters and creatures roam!" Willy announced. He seemed proud, as if he were the master of all that lived in the Dark Land. "The Titans, and the Arai, and Akhlys! So many dark creatures!"

"At the Doors of Death, there are even more monsters!" Philly said giddily. "A huge army of them! It's like a non-stop monster party!"

Great, Nico thought. An army of monsters. How would he close the Doors with a monster army guarding them?

His mission was doomed.

"We could show you through the Dark Lands," Willy offered. "I'll introduce you to my friends! My brother Ripper will be glad to eat you."

Philly whispered in Willy's ear, and Willy corrected himself. "I meant, he'll be glad to meet you."

No, Nico thought, you were right the first time.

Even so, he had to find the Doors of Death. If he didn't unchain them, the world would be plagued forever by a never-ending parade of monsters. And when heroes slayed the monsters, they would just use the Doors to return from the dead, like flowers coming back in the spring. It would be a disaster.

So," Willy asked, interrupting Nico's thoughts. "How's about it? Ready for a tour?"

"Well..."

"Come on, it'll be fun!" Philly said. "We can even hunt for that demigod that Gaea told everyone to find!"

Nico felt as though he'd been struck by lightning. "What? What demigod do you mean?"

"You don't know?" Philly looked shocked. "Some kid named Nico. There's a huge reward for anyone who finds him."

Gods, no! Nico's stomach sank. His face went cold. "What kind of reward?" he asked.

The cyclops shrugged. Philly answered for them. "She didn't say. We assume it's something delicious. Maybe a year's supply of demigod meatballs! Mmmm!"

The two cyclops rubbed their bulging stomachs dreamily.

Nico's throat closed up. For a moment, he couldn't breathe. He didn't understand why Gaea had told all the monsters in Tartarus to look for him.

Had he done something wrong, something that offended Gaea? All he'd ever done was to kill a few monsters and send them to Tartarus—nothing that any ordinary demigod wouldn't do.

Maybe they made a mistake, Nico thought hopefully. Cyclops were so stupid.

But if it was a mistake, how did they know his name?

"You okay there, buddy?" Willy asked. "You look a little gooey."

I'll bet I do, Nico thought grimly. "Why don't you guys show me around a little? Just so I don't get lost."

"Yes, yes!" The cyclops nodded enthusiastically. "A tour of Tartarus!" "All right then." Nico straightened up. "Let's get moving."

5

This is a bad idea. This is a bad idea. This is a bad idea.

That was all Nico could think as they walked. The two cyclops trudged ahead of him, with their giant "pet" alongside. The air seemed to grow hotter by the minute. The ground was full of jagged, spiky rocks. Every step hurt.

Inches from his feet, steep cliffs dropped away, with lakes of fiery lava surging below.

Nico thought longingly of his sister, Hazel. What would he give to be with her now, or with any of his friends — Percy, Annabeth, it didn't matter who.

"Time to meet our friends," Willy said.

Nico's head shot up. Friends?

Ahead of them, at the base of a towering cliff, stood a group of human- size figures. Nico saw one of them tilt its head curiously. As he approached, he heard hisses and sniggers. He kept his head down. He dreaded seeing what was awaiting him.

Eventually, though, he had no choice but to look up.

Gods of Olympus! Nico almost screamed. Seven women stood before him, except, they weren't quite human. Their left legs were bright bronze, while their right legs were furry and donkey-like. Their faces were pale as snow, their hair fiery red. When they opened their mouths, fangs as sharp as needles showed.

"What's this?" the girl in the torn cheerleader uniform asked. "Oh my gosh, Philly and Willy, you guys brought us a gift!"

"You—you're empousai!" Nico stammered. "Vampires..."

"That's right, and you're a demigod. I'll really enjoy sucking on your bones."

The two cyclops straightened up and waved their clubs wildly.

"No, Kelli!" Philly screeched. "He's not a demigod! That's just a disguise. This is our friend!"

"Don't lie to me, Philly!" Kelli snarled. "If he's not a demigod, then what is he? A monster?"

She threw her head back and gave a loud cackle. The other empousai did the same.

"It's his cologne that's fooling you!" Willy argued. Both cyclops seemed upset now, because
the empousai were laughing at them. "He wears this special cologne that makes him smell like a demigod."

Kelli stared at Nico with disgust. "You have got to be kidding me," she drawled. "You? A monster?" She took a step toward him. Her hands straightened into claws. "I'll tell you who you do look like, though: a lone, lost demigod. One who has a very high price on his head."

"I don't know what you're talking about," Nico said, backing away slowly.

"Oh please," Kelli snarled. The other empousai were slowly advancing upon

Nico as well. "You're obviously that stupid kid Gaea wants. Too bad she wants you alive. Otherwise, we would feast on your flesh."

"Stay back!" Nico shouted, pointing his sword at them. He called to Philly and Willy, "Help me, guys! Tell them I'm not a demigod!"

But the cyclops made no move. "Is it true, little one?" Willy asked sadly. "Did you lie to us?"

"No!" Nico screamed.

"Yes!" Kelly shrieked.

The two one-eyed faces turned dark with rage.

"You know, Philly," Willy said slowly through gritted teeth. "He doesn't look like a monster at all."

"No, he doesn't," Philly growled. "Maybe Kelli's right."

"Did you think you could trick us, boy?" Willy roared. "Did you think we're stupid? Well, I don't care if Gaea wants you alive! I will rip you apart, suck on your bones, and drink your blood. Then, I will bring what's left to Gaea."

The two cyclops moved forward, their clubs raised.

The whole scene was so overwhelming—the seven empousai advancing, the two cyclops roaring, the drakon lashing its tail—that Nico couldn't help himself, he screamed in terror.

"Stop!"

A different vampire, standing on a ledge above them, held out her gnarled, wrinkled hand. "If we kill the boy, Gaea will punish us. She clearly said that he was to be captured alive."

"But he tricked us!" Philly moaned.

"Think of the reward!" Kelli reminded him. "Oh. My. Gods. Gaea will give you so much food!"

"Yes!" both cyclops roared. "The food!" They raised their clubs higher. "Let's strike him on the head," Philly roared. "We'll bring his limp body to the Doors. That's where Gaea wants him, right?"

"Yes!" Willy roared. The two cyclops leaped forward and raised their clubs. Nico held out his sword, but knew it was no use.

"Stop!" Kelli screeched. The cyclops hesitated. "Oh my gosh, you guys. You didn't really think we would let you get the prize, did you?" She gave a sly smile. "Two stupid cyclops, getting all the glory for catching a demigod? I don't think so."

The cyclops slowly turned towards Kelli. Nico breathed a sigh of relief. For the moment, at least, he didn't have to worry about getting his skull bashed in.

With a sudden scream of rage, the cyclops rushed at the empousai. A few of the vampires managed to jump out of their reach, but the others weren't so lucky. Two were crushed by the cyclops' enormous bodies. They crumbled into the dust, wailing as they died.

"How dare you!" Kelli shrieked. Her hair was wild, her claws fully extended at the cyclops. She rushed at the cyclops, ready to draw blood, but Philly batted her aside with his club.

The rest of the empousai attacked together. The cyclops knocked them away as if they were grasshoppers. One empousai, however, was quicker than the rest. She dodged the heavy club and raked her claws against Philly's leg. He screamed.

"Bloodsucker!" Philly roared, his face red with rage. "Knock them out! All of them!" He whipped his club through the air, smacking another empousai. "But don't kill them," he snarled. "I want them to watch when I receive my prize from Gaea."

The drakon whipped his tail through the air, and used it to smack the remaining vampires on the head. Each girl crumpled as she was hit. Soon, five empousai were lying on the ground, their hair hanging over their faces. The drakon gave a triumphant roar.

"Good boy, Bloodsucker!" Willy shouted. "Now," he pointed his club at Nico. "Get that one too."

As the enormous drakon charged toward him, Nico turned and ran. Run, run, he told himself. But his lungs seemed to be broken; his legs felt as though they were made of iron.

Something behind him cut through the air and struck him on the head. And then he was falling. The last thing Nico saw as he collapsed was the reddish glow of fire rising from a river up ahead.

6

When Nico woke up, he found himself surrounded by monsters. He shut his eyes, trying to escape their hideous faces. He was being carried. Loud cheers sounded all around him. "Bring him to the Doors!" a voice shouted. \

Up ahead, two enormous black doors towered high. Thick chains held them closed. There could be no doubt: he had found the Doors of Death. The dog-like face of a telkhine came up close to his face and squeaked. "Hey, he's awake!" a winged hag hissed. "Bad demigod! Stay down!"

Nico recognized Philly's voice. The enormous cyclops held him. Then, a huge club came down. Everything turned black.

* * *

When Nico awoke this time, he was no longer in Tartarus. But he wasn't in a nice, comfy bed at Camp Half-Blood, either. He was curled on the ground in what looked like a huge parking garage. Rows of stone pillars held up the ceiling. Glowing braziers cast a dim light over the many pulleys, sandbags, and dark theater lights hanging above him. At the sides of the space, he could see moving machinery and water rushing through trenches.

Nico stood up and groaned. Every bone, every muscle ached. His head was pounding. He reached up and felt a swollen lump at the top of his temple. Even that gentle touch resulted in agony. Two giants entered, clutching enormous spears. They faced him with dark scowls on their identical faces. Both were about twelve feet tall. They wore matching outfits: black leather jackets, pink rubber pants, and snakes as shoes. The only difference between them was that one had long, purple dreadlocks while the other had green hair.

"Demigod!" the purple-haired giant roared. "I was starting to worry that you were dead." He gave a loud laugh, and his brother joined in.

"Who are you?" Nico asked.

The giant's lips curled into a vicious smile. "Who are we? Who are we, indeed! I am the spontaneous, the outrageous, the terrific Ephialtes!" He turned to the green-haired one. "And this is my brother, Otis."

"Otis the Magnificent!" the green-haired giant roared.

"Yes, yes, if you say so," Ephialtes said dismissively. "Otis, do you have the jar prepared?"

"The jar, yes, um, the jar..."

"Oh, gods, Otis! Can't you do anything right? Go get the jar and set it up!"

Otis scowled at his brother before turning away and rummaging through a pile of crates against the wall.

Meanwhile, Ephialtes watched Nico closely. Nico tried to stay calm and clear-headed, but it wasn't easy with a swelling lump on his head and two armed giants guarding him.

He noticed his sword on the ground a few feet away. With a cry of joy—followed by a moan because of the throbbing in his head—he leaped forward and grabbed it.

"Yes, yes, your little sword," Ephialtes said. "Useful for slicing cheese and meats, but not much else."

Nico pointed the sword at the giant. Although his insides were a bubbling pot of fear, he asked boldly, "What are you going to do with me?"

"Hold you hostage, of course," the giant said. "What, did you think we would kill you? That would be so... predictable. No, this is much better. When your seven friends come to rescue you"—he whipped his spear through the air—"we will destroy them all!"

"Yes! Destroy them!" Otis shouted, his head deep in a crate.

"And after that, we will destroy all the demigods in the world! Mother will be so pleased!" Ephialtes smiled, envisioning his triumph.

"Your mother?" Nico asked.

"Mother Gaea!" Ephialtes said happily. "She will be so pleased when we have destroyed Rome!"

"Rome! Is that where I am right now?" Nico asked.

"Yes, Rome. A young city, but fairly impressive, for humans." Ephialtes bounced on his feet. "Still, we will destroy it easily."

Nico was confused. How did he get to Rome? And how were these two giants going to destroy the city?

As if reading his thoughts, Ephialtes said, "You were brought here through the Doors of Death in Tartarus, to the mortal side in Epirus."

"That's in Greece!" Otis shouted, helpfully.

"Shut up!" Ephialtes roared. "Anyway, Gaea's monsters brought you here to serve as bait. Your seven demigod friends will, of course, come to rescue you. And then we will kill them." His raised his spear high and gave a loud roar.

"What friends are you talking about?" Nico shouted, panicked. "Hazel? Percy? Tell me!" Beneath his fear, he felt a surge of anger.

Ephialtes, however, remained unfazed. "How am I supposed to remember all their names? That's not important, anyway. All that matters is that they die."

"I found it!" Otis shouted. He had in his hands a jar made of bronze, big enough to hold a human or a demigod.

"Excellent!" Ephialtes roared. With one hand, he picked up Nico, sword and all. Otis stepped forward with the jar.

Nico struggled. "You're putting me in that?" he screamed.

"Of course, little demigod," Ephialtes said calmly. "I would have preferred something more exciting. Hanging you in hot iron chains, perhaps, or locking you in a cage with a hellhound. But Mother insisted on this."

Nico tried to slash Ephialtes's hand with his sword, but the giant had both of his arms pinned. Before Nico could move, the jar came down over him. All was darkness.

7

"No!" Nico yelled. He slammed against his curved bronze prison and slashed at it with his sword. "Let me out!" he bellowed.

If the giants heard him, they didn't care. Nico slumped to the ground, tears streaming down his face. This was all his fault. Why had he gone into Tartarus in the first place? How could he have thought for one moment that he could survive? Now he was caught, and his friends would lose their lives—all because of his foolishness. And Rome would be destroyed!

It became warm inside the bronze jar, and hard to breathe. Nico realized that the jar was sealed. If he didn't do something quickly, he would suffocate and die. He leaned his sword against the jar and dug in his pockets. It must be here, it must be here, he thought desperately.

Finally, when his lungs were screaming for air, he found what he was looking for. It was eight tiny pomegranate seeds from Persophone's magic garden. If he chewed them and spat them out, he could survive without air. Each seed was good for a few hours. He had kept them in his pocket ever since the goddess gave them to him.

But the giants might keep him here for weeks— until his friends arrived. Even with the magic seeds, he would need to conserve oxygen if he wanted to survive. That meant going into a death trance. Nico had never done this before, but he knew how. An old hag had taught him a couple months ago.

He had to close his eyes, lose all of his senses, and pull himself above and away from everything around him. Almost like he was meditating. Then, he sat down cross-legged and closed his eyes. Using the death trance, Nico estimated that he would be able to survive with one pomegranate seed a day.

Time moved at an agonizingly slow pace. Nico sat cross-legged in his trance. It required all of his concentration to stay in the trance, especially as the days passed and he grew weaker. When he was down to one seed, he prayed that his friends would find him and save him. Then he chewed the seed, spat it out, and returned to his trance.

He was concentrating on his trance when he discovered that he couldn't breathe. Opening his eyes, he reached for the seeds, but remembered there were none left. Nico slapped the wall, panicking. His lungs felt as though they were going to tear apart from the strain of seeking air.

Nico's only thought was of his friends: maybe they hadn't been killed. If they had, Ephialtes and Otis would have surely killed Nico too. He fell to the floor. Goodbye, he thought. The world turned black. Nico closed his eyes and let go of everything.

8

"Nico, Nico!"

Who was that? The voice sounded so familiar.

"Nico, wake up!"

Nico opened his eyes. His head was resting on someone's lap. Above him were a pair of familiar copper eyes. His sister, Hazel, stroked his hair.

"You found me," Nico whispered. He felt a flutter of relief. "Hazel, I was in Tartarus. I almost died…"

"What?" Hazel gasped. "What do you mean?"

"Where am I, Hazel?" Nico asked.

Hazel smiled at him. She hugged him and laughed. Nico thought he had never heard anything as beautiful.

"You're safe now, Nico," she told him. "Whether you went to Tartarus or not, you're safe now. That's all that matters."

About The Author

Caroline Gee is a young writer. She loves to read and play sports. Some of her favorite authors are John Green, J.K. Rowling, and Rick Riordan. Caroline contributed to the Storyshares organization because she thought it would be a fun experience and for a good cause.

About The Publisher

Story Shares is a nonprofit focused on supporting the millions of teens and adults who struggle with reading by creating a new shelf in the library specifically for them. The ever-growing collection features content that is compelling and culturally relevant for teens and adults, yet still readable at a range of lower reading levels.

Story Shares generates content by engaging deeply with writers, bringing together a community to create this new kind of book. With more intriguing and approachable stories to choose from, the teens and adults who have fallen behind are improving their skills and beginning to discover the joy of reading. For more information, visit storyshares.org.

Easy to Read. Hard to Put Down.

Deep in the Underworld